Learning to Fly

Text and illustrations
by Sebastian Meschenmoser

Kane/Miller
BOOK PUBLISHERS

Last winter, I found a penguin.

He told me he'd been flying.
But…penguins can't fly.

He knew that.
But, penguins are birds, and birds fly, so...

...he gave it a try. And, he flew.

Then he met some other birds.

They said, "Penguins can't fly."
And he thought, "They're right."

That's when he crashed.

He looked so heartbroken that I believed him.

Then I took him home.

I gave him something to eat.

And found him a place to sleep.

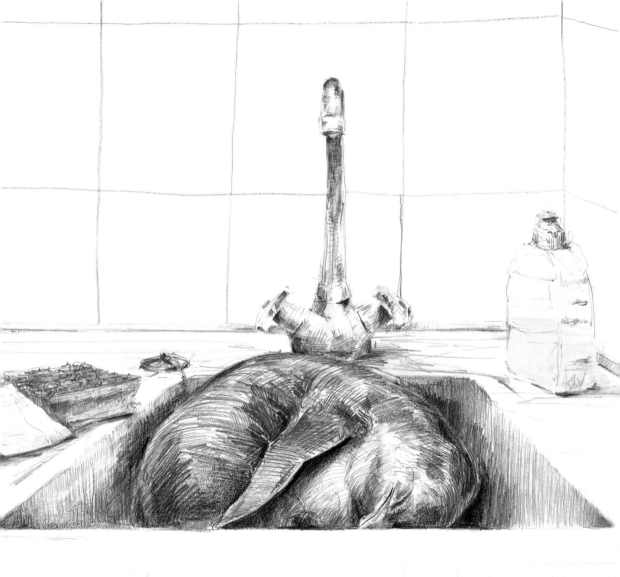

The next morning, we realized it was true.
Penguins really can't fly.

I began to test his aerodynamics,

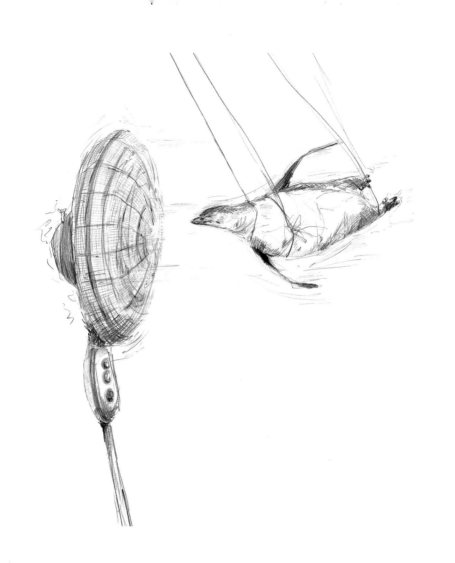

and his body stress levels.

We set up a training program.

We even studied books about flying.

We came up with some good ideas.

And some not so good ideas.

After that, we began to practice…

...mostly outside.

We tried almost everything.

But, nothing seemed to work.

One day, while working on something brand new,
we heard a strange noise.

A penguin colony was flying overhead.

Suddenly, my penguin stretched out his wings,
pushed off, and joined them in the air.

He flew pretty well…

…for a penguin.

WITHDRAWN